Circus
Fun

DEAR CAREGIVER,

The books in this Beginning-to-Read collection may look somewhat familiar in that the original versions could have been a part of your own early reading experiences. These carefully written texts feature common sight words to provide your child multiple exposures to the words appearing most frequently in written text. These new versions have been updated and the engaging illustrations are highly appealing to a contemporary audience of young readers.

Begin by reading the story to your child, followed by letting him or her read familiar words and soon your child will be able to read the story independently. At each step of the way, be sure to praise your reader's efforts to build his or her confidence as an independent reader. Discuss the pictures and encourage your child to make connections between the story and his or her own life. At the end of the story, you will find reading activities and a word list that will help your child practice and strengthen beginning reading skills. These activities, along with the comprehension questions are aligned to current standards, so reading efforts at home will directly support the instructional goals in the classroom.

Above all, the most important part of the reading experience is to have fun and enjoy it!

Shannon Cannon

Shannon Cannon,
Literacy Consultant

Norwood House Press • www.norwoodhousepress.com
Beginning-to-Read™ is a registered trademark of Norwood House Press.
Illustration and cover design copyright ©2017 by Norwood House Press. All Rights Reserved.

Authorized adapted reprint from the U.S. English language edition, entitled Circus Fun by Margaret Hillert. Copyright © 2017 Pearson Education, Inc. or its affiliates. Reprinted with permission. All rights reserved. Pearson and Circus Fun are trademarks, in the US and/or other countries, of Pearson Education, Inc. or its affiliates. This publication is protected by copyright, and prior permission to re-use in any way in any format is required by both Norwood House Press and Pearson Education. This book is authorized in the United States for use in schools and public libraries.

Designer: Lindaanne Donohoe
Editorial Production: Lisa Walsh

LIBRARY OF CONGRESS CATALOGING-IN-PUBLICATION DATA
Names: Hillert, Margaret, author. I Masheris, Robert, illustrator.
Title: Circus fun / by Margaret Hillert ; illustrated by Bob Masheris.
Description: Chicago, IL : Norwood House Press, [2016] I Series: A
  Beginning-to-Read book I Summary: "A boy spends the day at the circus, and
  sees all the attractions including a parade, the big top tent, clowns and
  acrobats"-- Provided by publisher.
Identifiers: LCCN 2016002598 (print) I LCCN 2016022107 (ebook) I ISBN
  9781599537962 (library edition : alk. paper) I ISBN 9781603579582 (eBook)
Subjects: I CYAC: Circus--Fiction.
Classification: LCC PZ7.H558 Ci 2016 (print) I LCC PZ7.H558 (ebook) I DDC
  [E]--dc23
LC record available at https://lccn.loc.gov/2016002598

288N—072016
Manufactured in the United States of America in North Mankato, Minnesota.

Margaret Hillert's

Circus
Fun

A Beginning-to-Read Book

Illustrated by Bob Masheris

Oh, Father, look, look.
Here is something funny.
I want to go to it.

Father said, "Come, come.
We can go.
Run, run, run."

I see it.
Here it is.
We go in here.

Here is something big.
Big, big, big!

They make it go up.
Up, up, up!
Oh, my.
We want to go in.

I see something.
I want one.
Father, can I get one?

Here we go, Father.
Up here, up here.
Help me go up!

Oh, look, look.
One little one.
Two big ones.
See the pretty ball.
The little one can play ball.

See something funny.
They can go up.
They can come down.
Up and down.
Up and down.

Oh, oh, oh.
Look up here.
Look up and up and up.

And look down there.
Here is something fun.
It can go, go go.

Here is a funny one.
I see three balls.
Red, yellow, and blue balls.

Oh, oh.
Where is the red ball?
Where is the yellow ball?
Where is the blue ball?

Here is one.
Here is one.
And—here is one.

See my funny car.
Come into my funny car.
We can go away in it.
Away, away, away.

Look here.
See the big father.
See the big mother.
See the little baby.

They can go up.
Up, up, up.
Up they go.

Oh, Father, Father.
Look. Look.
What fun!

Down.
Down.
Down they go.

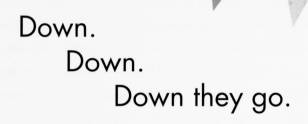

Mother, Mother.
Look here.
Here is something for you.

And here is a cookie for you.
Cookies for you and Father.

Foundational Skills

In addition to reading the numerous high-frequency words in the text, this book also supports the development of foundational skills.

Phonological Awareness: The soft c sound

Oral Blending: Explain to your child that sometimes the letter **c** makes the same sound as **s**. Say the beginning and ending parts of the following words and ask your child to listen to the sounds and say the whole word:

/c/ + ircus = circus	/c/ + ity = city	/c/ + ent = cent
/c/ + ereal = cereal	/c/ + ircle = circle	/c/ + elery = celery
/c/ + enter = center	/c/ + ement = cement	

Phonics: The letters c, e, and i

1. Demonstrate how to form the letters **c**, **e**, and **i** for your child.
2. Have your child practice writing **c**, **e**, and **i** at least three times each.
3. Point to the word Circus on the front cover. Explain to your child that when **c** is followed by the letters **i** or **e**, it sounds like /**s**/.
4. Ask your child to point to the words in the story that begin with the letter **c**. Ask your child if they are followed by the letters **e** or **i**.
5. Write the following spaces and letters on a piece of paper. Say the complete word and help your child decide whether the spaces should be filled with the letters **c-e** or **c-i**. Ask your child to write the correct letters in the spaces:

__ __ty	__ __nt	__ __rcus	__ __lery
__ __rcle	__ __nter	__ __real	__ __ment

6. Ask your child to read each completed word. Provide help sounding them out as needed.

Fluency: Echo Reading

1. Reread the story to your child at least two more times while your child tracks the print by running a finger under the words as they are read. Ask your child to read the words he or she knows with you.
2. Reread the story, stopping after each sentence or page to allow your child to read (echo) what you have read. Repeat echo reading and let your child take the lead.

Language

The concepts, illustrations, and text in this book help children develop language both explicitly and implicitly.

Vocabulary: Circus Words

1. Write the following words on separate pieces of sticky note paper and point to them as you read them to your child:

   clowns   cars   dogs   balloons   horses   tent

2. Mix the words up. Say each word in random order and ask your child to point to the correct word as you say it.
3. Mix the words up and ask your child to read as many as he or she can.
4. Ask your child to place the sticky notes on the correct page for each word that describes something in the story.

Reading Literature and Informational Text

To support comprehension, ask your child the following questions. The answers either come directly from the text or require inferences and discussion.

Key Ideas and Detail

- Ask your child to retell the sequence of events in the story.
- Who are the people who work in the circus?

Craft and Structure

- Is this a book that tells a story or one that gives information? How do you know?
- Do you think the boy had fun at the circus? Why?

Integration of Knowledge and Ideas

- If you could be in a circus, what would you like to do?
- Have you ever been to the circus? If so, what was your favorite part? If not, do you think you would like to go to the circus?

WORD LIST

Circus Fun uses the 53 words listed below.

This list can be used to practice reading the words that appear in the text. You may wish to write the words on index cards and use them to help your child build automatic word recognition. Regular practice with these words will enhance your child's fluency in reading connected text.

a	Father	little	red	want(s)
and	for	look	run	we
away	fun			what
	funny	make	said	where
baby		me	see	
ball(s)	get	Mother	something	yellow
big	go	my		you
blue			the	
	help	oh	there	
can	here	one(s)	they	
car			three	
come	I	play	to	
cookie(s)	in	pretty	two	
	into			
down	is		up	
	it			

ABOUT THE AUTHOR Margaret Hillert has helped millions of children all over the world learn to read independently. She was a first grade teacher for 34 years and during that time started writing books that her students could both gain confidence in reading and enjoy. She wrote well over 100 books for children just learning to read. As a child, she enjoyed writing poetry and continued her poetic writings as an adult for both children and adults.

Photograph by Glenna Washburn

ABOUT THE ILLUSTRATOR A talented and creative artist, Robert Masheris is a graduate of Bradley University. He began his career as a watercolor artist and with the advent of the computer age began to provide his illustrations in the digital form. Robert has illustrated numerous delightful children's books, educational materials, and artist's prints. Robert currently resides in Illinois.